Note to parents, carers and teachers

Read it yourself is a series of modern stories, favourite characters, traditional tales and first reference books written in a simple way for children who are learning to read. The books can be read independently or as part of a guided reading session.

Each book is carefully structured to include many high-frequency words vital for first reading. The sentences on each page are supported closely by pictures to help with understanding, and to offer lively details to talk about.

The books are graded into four levels that progressively introduce wider vocabulary and longer text as a reader's ability and confidence grows.

Ideas for use

• Ask how your child would like to approach reading at this stage. Would he prefer to hear you read the book first, or would he like to read the words to you and see how he gets on?

• Help him to sound out any words he does not know.

• Developing readers can be concentrating so hard on the words that they sometimes don't fully grasp the meaning of what they're reading. Answering the quiz questions at the end of the book will help with understanding.

For more information and advice on Read it yourself and book banding, visit **www.ladybird.com/readityourself**

Book Band 7

Level 3 is ideal for children who are developing reading confidence and stamina, and who are eager to read longer books with a wider vocabulary.

Special features:

Wider vocabulary, reinforced through repetition

Simple story structure

Alex and the A-Stars were a rock band.

"Let's enter the talent show!" said Alex.

Alex and the A-Stars practised their music all day.

Longer sentences

In the final, the A-Stars played their new song first. Everyone cheered.

Next, the Zigzags did their new dance and everyone cheered again.

So who were the winners? Mr West announced, "The winners are . . ."

Detailed pictures for added interest and discussion

26

27

Educational Consultant: Geraldine Taylor
Book Banding Consultant: Kate Ruttle

LADYBIRD BOOKS

UK | USA | Canada | Ireland | Australia
India | New Zealand | South Africa

Ladybird Books is part of the Penguin Random House group of companies
whose addresses can be found at global.penguinrandomhouse.com.

www.penguin.co.uk   www.puffin.co.uk   www.ladybird.co.uk

Penguin
Random House
UK

First published 2017
This edition 2019
002

Copyright © Ladybird Books Ltd, 2017

Printed in China

A CIP catalogue record for this book is available from the British Library

ISBN: 978-0-241-40540-6

All correspondence to:
Ladybird Books
Penguin Random House Children's
One Embassy Gardens, 8 Viaduct Gardens, London SW11 7BW

The Talent Show

Written by Mandy Ross

Illustrated by Ryan Wheatcroft

Harmony School was the biggest school in Bridge Town.

"It's time to find some new talent in Harmony School," said Mr West. "Let's have a talent show."

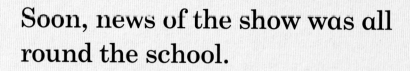

Soon, news of the show was all round the school.

"The Harmony School talent show starts soon," announced Mr West.

Alex and the A-Stars were
a rock band.

"Let's enter the talent show!"
said Alex.

Alex and the A-Stars practised
their music all day.

Ziggy and the Zigzags were
a street dance act.

"We can win the talent show!"
said Ziggy.

Ziggy and the Zigzags practised
all day, too.

It was the first round of the talent show. Harmony School had a lot of talent – not just music and dance!

Everyone clapped and cheered all the acts.

The A-Stars and the Zigzags
both did well in that round.

Everyone clapped and cheered!

The A-Stars and the Zigzags both
made it to the final!

The Zigzags had a new dance
for the final.

"The Zigzags' new dance is cool!"
said Alex. "But we can't let them
win. We must practise some more."

19

The A-Stars had a new song to play in the final.

"The A-Stars rock!" said Ziggy. "Hey, Zigzags, if we want to win, we must practise even more."

The next day, Alex saw
Ziggy on the way to school.

"Hey, Ziggy," said Alex. "Your
street dance is cool, but you can
tell that everyone loves rock music
even more."

Ziggy saw Alex at school.

"Hey, Alex," said Ziggy. "Your rock band is cool, but I tell you, everyone loves street dance even more."

In the final, the A-Stars played their new song first. Everyone cheered.

Next, the Zigzags did their new dance and everyone cheered again.

So who were the winners? Mr West announced, "The winners are . . ."

. . . the Zigzags!" Everyone cheered the Zigzags.

Alex and the A-Stars cheered the Zigzags, too.

The next day, Mr West announced, "It is time for the Bridge Town talent show to start."

Soon, news of the Bridge Town talent show was all round Harmony School.

"This is another chance to win!"
Alex said to the A-Stars. "We must
find something extra. Maybe we
need some dancers . . ."

"This is our chance to win again!"
Ziggy said to the Zigzags. "We must
find something extra this time. We
need to tell a story. Maybe we need
some new music . . ."

Ziggy saw Alex on the way home from school.

"Hey . . ." said Ziggy.

"Hey . . ." said Alex.

"The A-Stars rock! We want you to play with us," said Ziggy.

"And we love your act! We want you to dance with us!" said Alex.

And so the A-Stars and the Zigzags made one big, new act – the A-Star Zigzags.

The A-Stars played their music and the Zigzags danced.

They were big news!

41

The A-Star Zigzags entered the
Bridge Town talent show.

They practised again and again
all day . . . and all the next day.

It was the first round of the Bridge Town talent show.

The A-Star Zigzags danced and played. Everyone cheered, but who were the winners?

Well, that's another story . . .

How much do you remember about the story of The Talent Show? Answer these questions and find out!

- What is the name of the school?

- Who announces that there will be a talent show?

- What sort of act are the A-Stars?

- Who wins the school talent show?

- Who enters the Bridge Town talent show?

Look at the **different story sentences and match them to the characters who said them.**

"We must find something extra. Maybe we need some dancers . . ."

"Your rock band is cool, but I tell you, everyone loves street dance even more."

"It is time for the Bridge Town talent show to start."

www.ladybird.com